LADYBIRD BOOKS, INC.
Auburn, Maine 04210 U.S.A.
© LADYBIRD BOOKS LTD 1991
Loughborough, Leicestershire, England

Printed in England (3)

Little Bunnies At Home

By Norma Daniels
Illustrated by Carolyn Bracken

Ladybird Books

The Bunny Family

brother

sister

This is Billy Bunny.   This is his sister, Betsy.

And this is the rest of their family.

Friends and Neighbors

This is where Billy and Betsy live.

house

weather vane

ranch house

sewer drain

streetlight

garbage can

sidewalk

garage door

Their friend Henry Bear lives next door.

Francine Fox lives in the tall building.

And Dan Kitten lives at the corner.

fire hydrant

apartment house

litter basket

town house

traffic light

mailbox

The Bunnies' House
Here is Billy and Betsy's house.

roof

window

porch

door

letter slot

yard

shrubs

chimney

Who is peeking out the window?

window box

garage

rake

tire

steps

tricycle

bicycle

car

path

driveway

The Back Yard

hose

shovel

trowel

hoe

fork

vegetable garden

barbecue grill

patio

sandbox

Billy and Betsy are playing with their friends in the back yard.

Can you find the ball?

flower garden

lawn mower

nest

swing

tire swing

The Kitchen

range hood

cabinets

potholder

bowls

oven

microwave

canisters

toaster

stove

plates

napkins

oven
mitt

Everyone helps out in the kitchen.

freezer

sink

coffee maker

food processor

dishwasher

dustpan

cake stand

brush

refrigerator

spilled raisins

There's certainly a lot to do!

The Dining Room
It's lunchtime.

highchair

bib

table

ladle

glass

soup

butter

spoon

soup tureen

tablecloth

Betsy loves vegetable soup, but Billy
can't wait for dessert!

The Living Room

picture

fireplace

lamp

plant

furniture polish

throw pillow

television/TV

rug

electrical outlet

couch/sofa

Billy and Henry are trying to watch television.

armchair

But they can't hear very much!

The Attic

On rainy days, Billy and Betsy and their friends play in the attic.

peacock feathers

birdcage

vase

hangers

golf clubs

trunk

old clothes

light bulb

tennis racket

Who's under the big hat?

cracked mirror

dressmaker's dummy

hatbox

storage box

The Basement

poster

Ping-Pong table

paddle

bleach

fabric softener

laundry detergent

washing machine

dryer

Betsy and Billy like to help with the laundry.

darts

dartboard

spray starch

iron

screwdriver

hammer

saw

file

toolbox

vise

stool

nails

ironing board

drill

workbench

laundry basket

wastebasket

Sam likes to ride in the basket!

The Baby's Room

cotton swabs   baby lotion

cotton balls   baby powder

rattle

pacifier

changing table

diaper pail

diaper

Mom is putting Sam to bed. Billy helps
her change his diaper.

What can you see under Sam's crib?

rocking chair

mobile

bottle

top   blocks

toy chest

crib

The Bathroom
It's bathtime.

towel

light switch

bathrobe

toilet

toilet paper

clothes hamper

tissues

radiator

Betsy is nearly dry,
but Billy is still
sailing his boats.

medicine cabinet

shaving cream

mouthwash

toothpaste

sink

toothbrushes

shower

shower cap

tap   faucet

rubber duck

sponge

ubble bath   soap

boats

bathtub

The Bedroom

kite

model airplane

mirror

comb

brush

dresser

teddy bear

alarm clock

blanket

nightstand

quilt

At bedtime, Mom tucks Billy and Betsy in, and Dad reads them a story.

rocking horse

doll

pillow

clothes closet

moon

book

bed

bookcase

slippers

Good night, little Bunnies. Sleep tight!

BILLY BETSY

DAD SAM MOM